Kathryn

the Gym
Fairy

To Iona and Lowena

Special thanks to Rachel Elliot

ISBN 978-0-545-85208-1

10 9 8 7 6 5 4 3 2 1   16 17 18 19 20

Printed in the U.S.A.   40
First edition, July 2016

Kathryn
the Gym
Fairy

by Daisy Meadows

SCHOLASTIC INC.

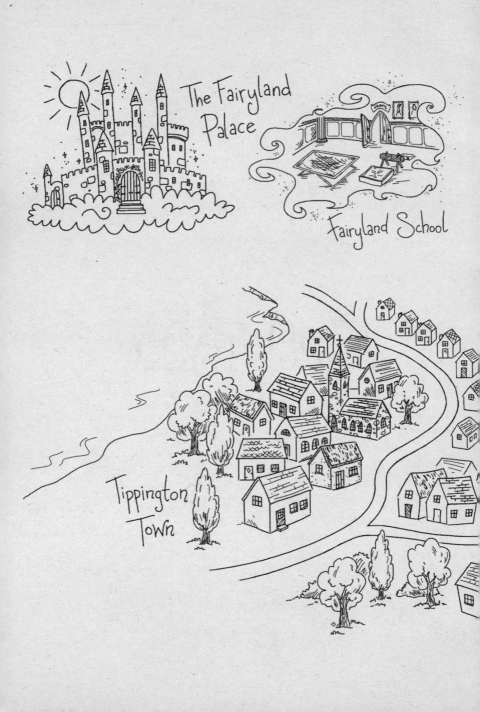

The Fairyland Palace

Fairyland School

Tippington Town

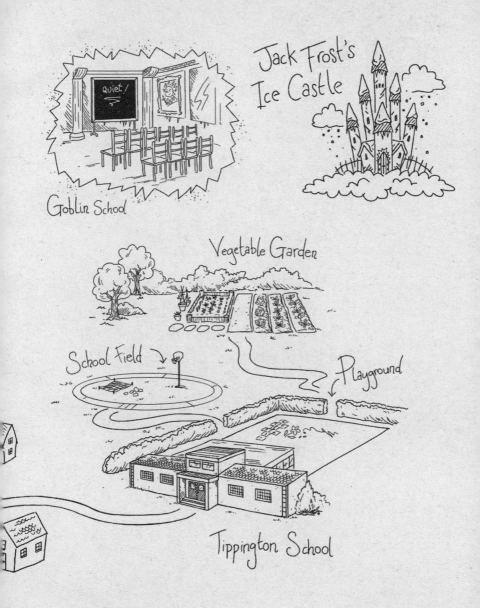

Goblin School

Jack Frost's Ice Castle

Vegetable Garden

School Field

Playground

Tippington School

It's time the School Day Fairies see
How wonderful a school should be—
A place where goblins must be bossed,
And learn about the great Jack Frost.

Now every fairy badge of gold
Makes goblins do as they are told.
Let silly fairies whine and wail.
My cleverness will never fail!

Contents

The School Superintendent

"I can't believe that tomorrow is our last day at school together," said Kirsty Tate. "It's been a wonderful week—I wish it didn't have to end."

Rachel Walker squeezed her hand as they sat next to each other in the auditorium. The best friends had loved every moment of the past week. Kirsty's school had been flooded, so she had joined Rachel in Tippington.

"It's good that your school will be open again next week, but I am going to miss you so much!" said Rachel.

They were sitting with the rest of Mr. Beaker's class at the afternoon assembly. Miss Patel, the principal, clapped her hands together and everyone fell silent.

"Good afternoon, everyone," she said. "I hope that you have all had a good morning and are looking forward to class this afternoon."

"Yes, Miss Patel!" all the students said together.

"Some of you have already met our school superintendent, Mrs. Best," Miss Patel went on. "She is observing the school today and tomorrow."

A lady with a clipboard joined Miss Patel at the front of the auditorium, and everyone clapped politely.

"I hope that you will all continue to show Mrs. Best what a wonderful school this is," said Miss Patel.

Just then, Rachel and Kirsty heard the sound of chattering nearby. They peered along their row and saw two boys in green uniforms, snickering and muttering to each other. The girls exchanged a knowing glance. They knew that the boys were goblins in disguise.

Miss Patel made a few short announcements and then sent everyone off to their classrooms.

"Look," Kirsty whispered, peering over her shoulder. "Mrs. Best is following our class."

Rachel looked, too, and saw Mrs. Best a few steps behind them.

"She must be coming to observe our gym class," said Rachel.

"I hope that the goblins behave themselves," said Kirsty in a low voice. "It would be awful if they messed things up for Tippington School."

Feeling anxious, the girls changed quickly into their shorts, T-shirts, and sneakers. Then they jogged out to the field with their friends Adam and Amina and the rest of the class.

Mrs. Best was waiting for them at the edge of the field, holding a clipboard. Mr. Beaker was standing beside her, and the girls saw him glancing down at the clipboard.

"Oh, I hope this class goes well," said Rachel, crossing her fingers. "Poor Mr. Beaker looks worried."

The goblins were at the back of the group, fooling around. Just as they had refused to wear the Tippington school uniform, they had also refused to wear the gym uniform. While everyone else matched in their navy-and-white uniforms, the goblins were dressed in scruffy, bright-green shorts and stained green T-shirts. They were wearing green baseball caps to hide their faces. Kirsty spotted Mrs. Best making notes on the clipboard, and her heart sank.

"Good afternoon, everyone," said Mr. Beaker, talking in an extra-cheerful voice. "We're going to do an obstacle-course relay, so I'd like you to get into teams of four, please."

"Will you two be on our team?" Rachel asked Adam and Amina.

Their friends agreed at once. There weren't quite enough children for everyone to have a team of four, so Mr. Beaker told the goblins that they could be a team and do two obstacles each.

Mr. Beaker led the children to the course. It looked like a lot of fun. There were all sorts of obstacles and challenges, with bean bags, balls, and cones laid out in a different color for each team.

"You'll all decide who on your team will go first, second, third, and fourth," Mr. Beaker explained. "The first person has to balance a bean bag on their head and weave through the line of cones. The second person must throw a basketball through the hoop. The third person needs to jump rope twenty times, and the fourth person must finish the relay by crawling under a low net to the finish line. When each person finishes their part of the course, they have to tag the next team member as the signal to go. Do you all understand?"

Rachel and Kirsty nodded, feeling very excited. They couldn't wait to get started!

Gym Class Problems

"This is a tough course, so it's important to practice first," said Mr. Beaker. "I'll give you all five minutes to discuss with your teams and then we'll begin."

Rachel and Kirsty's team decided that Amina would go first, Adam second, Kirsty third, and Rachel fourth. Their team color was purple, so Amina picked up a purple bean bag and set off around the cones.

"Wait!" cried Kirsty. "You're going the wrong way!"

But Amina didn't hear her, because all the teams were yelling at the tops of their lungs. The bean bag slipped off Amina's head and she picked it up, but she had only gone a few steps before it fell off again.

"Noooo!" cried Adam.

Suddenly Amina realized that she was going the wrong way around the cones. She turned around and headed back in the opposite

direction, and then the bean bag slipped off her head again. Adam groaned and the girls bit their lips. They couldn't help but notice that the first goblin had already reached the end of the cones. Somehow he had managed to balance the bean bag on his hat without dropping it once!

At last Amina reached the end of the cones and ran over to tag Adam. He sprinted toward the bucket full of basketballs and grabbed a purple one. He aimed it at the basketball hoop, but it went straight up in the air and came down on his head.

"Ow!" he yelled.

He grabbed the ball and aimed it at the basket again. This time it flew over the top of the basket and hit the second goblin on the shoulder. He was fiddling with one of his sneakers, and he gave a loud squawk. The ball bounced away into a muddy ditch.

"This is strange," said Amina. "Adam's really good at basketball—he usually never misses a shot!"

The second goblin had fixed his sneaker and then thrown the basketball through the hoop on his first try, but Adam had to try six times before he succeeded. Red in the face, he tagged Kirsty, who picked up a jump rope. She was usually good at jumping rope, but after just five jumps, the rope got tangled around her legs. *I guess I didn't jump high enough*, she thought. But when she tried again, she dropped one of the handles.

"You can do it, Kirsty!" Rachel called in an encouraging voice.

Kirsty picked up the rope to try again. But after fifteen jumps the rope hit the back of her head, and she lost her balance. She felt her cheeks turning red. The first goblin was next to her, pulling at one of his sneakers. Then he started jumping so fast that the rope was just a blur.

"What's wrong with me today?" Kirsty muttered under her breath.

She looked around to see if the other teams were looking at her, but to her surprise, they all looked just as confused and worried. Everyone was having problems with the obstacle course! One team was still on the bean bag section.

Kirsty took a deep breath and concentrated on jumping. This time she managed to reach twenty, although she tripped over her own feet when she ran over to tag Rachel. She glimpsed Mrs. Best shaking her head and making more notes on her clipboard.

Even though the goblins had finished jumping rope first, they were both doing something with their sneakers.

"It's lucky they don't have lace-up sneakers to slow them down," said Kirsty.

Rachel and the second goblin dived under the low net at exactly the same time. Rachel dragged herself along on her elbows. This was something that she had done many times, but suddenly she felt as if she had forgotten how to crawl. Her elbows ached, and the finish line seemed to be miles away. The second goblin was already a long way ahead of her.

Suddenly Rachel felt a tug on her foot, and realized that one of her sneakers was caught in the netting. Nearby, she could see other children having problems, too. Some of them were still on the basketball challenge. Mrs. Best was shaking her head again and taking even more notes.

Just then, the goblin scrambled under the finish line and jumped up and down, cheering. Mrs. Best smiled for the first time, and Rachel heard her speak to Mr. Beaker.

"At least *some* of your students are satisfactory," she said. "Those boys in green are excellent."

Rachel looked at her foot. It was so tangled in the netting that she knew she couldn't get it out by herself.

"Mr. Beaker," she called out. "I'm stuck."

Mr. Beaker came to help her, and Mrs. Best followed him.

"It's almost as if they've never had a gym class before," she said. "What have you been teaching them?"

Mr. Beaker helped Rachel to her feet, looking flustered.

"They have regular classes," he told the inspector. "They *all* have satisfactory gym skills—I don't understand what's going wrong today."

"We're usually much better," said Rachel. "Please, will you give us another chance?"

Mrs. Best looked at her watch.

"It's almost time to go," she said. "I will give your class another chance first thing tomorrow morning. I hope things will have improved by then!"

Gloating Goblins

Mrs. Best strode back toward the school, and Mr. Beaker sighed.

"All right, class," he said. "Let's clean up the course."

Most of the children wanted to help, but the goblins just kept messing around, giggling and shoving each other. Mr. Beaker didn't seem to notice.

"Rachel and Kirsty, could you straighten up the cones, please?" he asked.

The girls jogged over to the cones and started to put them back in line.

"What an awful gym class," said Kirsty. "I hope that we can do better tomorrow— Mr. Beaker looked really upset."

Rachel didn't reply, because she had just seen something very strange. A faint golden

glow was coming from underneath
one of the purple cones. She nudged
Kirsty, who lifted up the cone to look
underneath it. They heard the sound of a
tiny whistle, and then Kathryn the Gym
Fairy fluttered out
and waved at
them.

"Hello, girls!"
she called.

She was
wearing white
jeans decorated
with pink hearts,
a pink varsity jacket,
and a pretty pink ribbon
in her hair.

"Hello, Kathryn," said Kirsty. "What
are you doing here?"

"Queen Titania was watching your class in her Seeing Pool," Kathryn explained. "It went badly because the goblins have my magical gold star badge. I've come to ask for your help."

At the beginning of the week, Kirsty and Rachel had met Marissa the Science Fairy, one of the School Day Fairies. She had asked them to help her find her magical gold star badge, which naughty Jack Frost had stolen. The girls found out that he had taken the badges for four subjects—Science, Art, Reading, and Gym. He was planning to start his own school for goblins, and teach them all about himself!

Without the badges, lessons had turned into a disaster in both the human world and Fairyland. But the worst thing was that Queen Titania and King Oberon were coming to look around the Fairyland School. Unless the fairies got their magical star badges back, the royal visit would be ruined!

Rachel, Kirsty, and Marissa found out that Jack Frost had expelled two misbehaving goblins from his school, and that they had stolen the magical gold star badges from *him*. These were the goblins at Tippington School.

Rachel smiled at Kathryn.

"We've found the badges that belong to Marissa the Science Fairy, Alison the Art Fairy, and Lydia the Reading Fairy," she said. "I'm sure we can help you find yours, too!"

"Rachel! Kirsty!" called Mr. Beaker. "It's almost time for the bell. Please join the rest of the class."

Quickly, Kathryn darted into the pocket of Kirsty's gym shirt. The girls hurried over to join the other students.

"Before you all go and get changed, I want to talk about

tomorrow," said Mr. Beaker. "There was only one team who managed to finish the obstacle course today—well done, boys."

The goblins snickered, but everyone else looked very glum.

"It's really important for the school that we do well in front of Mrs. Best in the morning," said Mr. Beaker. "Could you please all try to memorize the rules tonight, and practice at home if you

can? Remember, the first person has to
weave through the line of cones with a
bean bag on his or her head. The second
person throws the basketball through
the hoop. The third person must jump
rope twenty times, and then the fourth
person crawls under the net to the finish
line. Don't forget to tag the next team
member as the signal to go."

"We'll do our best to make everything
all right tomorrow, sir," said Kirsty.

Mr. Beaker gave her a worried smile.

"All I ask is that you do your best,"
he said. "Now, I have asked today's
winning team to give you all a
demonstration."

Puffing out their chests and looking
very smug, the goblins stepped forward.
Rachel suddenly realized that if everyone

was watching the goblins, they wouldn't notice if she and Kirsty slipped away.

There were some spare cones stacked up behind them. As the first goblin set off with the bean bag on his head, Rachel pulled her best friend's arm and ducked down behind the cones.

"This is our chance to find out where the goblins are hiding Kathryn's magical badge," she whispered. "Kathryn, could you turn us into fairies? Then we can watch the goblins really closely without being seen."

The fairy had poked her head over the edge of Kirsty's T-shirt pocket, and now she pulled out her wand.

"I'm glad you're going to be fairy-sized for a while," she said with a smile. "It means that I can give you a real hug!"

Rachel and Kirsty grinned at one another as Kathryn waved her wand in the air.

The Dirty Ditch

Rachel and Kirsty felt themselves spinning and shrinking, and when they caught their breath they were as tiny as Kathryn, with delicate gossamer wings fluttering from their shoulders. The three little fairies hugged each other.

"I'm so glad to have you with me," said Kathryn. "I wouldn't have any idea how to get my badge back by myself."

"Don't worry," said Rachel. "If we all choose a place to hide on the obstacle course, I'm sure we'll see something that will give us a clue."

"Good idea," said Kirsty. "I'll go under the net."

"I'll hide on the basketball hoop," Rachel replied. "What about you, Kathryn?"

"I'll slip behind one of the cones," said the fairy. "The first goblin has almost finished—I'd better hurry!"

She zoomed toward the first part of the obstacle course and landed behind a cone, making

sure that none of the students could see
her. They were all watching the first
goblin, who reached the end of the cones
and tipped the bean bag off his head,
laughing. Kathryn watched him run up
to the second goblin and tag him. Both
goblins bent down for a moment as if to
check their sneakers,
but Kirsty could
see what they
were really
doing. The
second
goblin
tucked
something
golden into his
sneaker and then
sprinted over to the basketball challenge.

"Was that my badge?" Kathryn wondered aloud.

The second goblin made a basket with ease, bent down to pull at his left sneaker, and then tagged the first goblin. Watching from the basket, Rachel could see that he had passed a gold star-shaped badge to the first goblin.

"Kathryn's badge!" she said with a gasp.

With the badge tucked carefully inside one of his sneakers, the first goblin easily jumped rope twenty times. Kirsty was hiding under the low net, and she saw him pass the badge back to the second goblin.

"That's cheating!" she exclaimed.

She felt so annoyed that she forgot about hiding from the goblin, and he saw her as he dived under the finish line.

"Fairies!" he squawked.

At exactly the same moment, the school bell rang in the distance.

"Thank you for a wonderful demonstration, boys," said Mr. Beaker. "Good luck tomorrow, everyone. Now hurry back inside and get changed—it's time to go home!"

As Mr. Beaker and the other students hurried away, the goblin swiped at Kirsty with his long, bony fingers.

She dodged his hand and zoomed away toward the muddy ditch where Adam's basketball had gone earlier.

"Come back!" squealed the goblin.

He chased her, closely followed by Rachel and Kathryn. Kirsty flew as fast as she could, gasping for breath. If she could reach the ditch and fly over it, maybe the goblin would run into it without looking!

Kirsty flew over the ditch, but the goblin stopped on the edge.

"I'm not getting my sneakers dirty for a silly little fairy!" he grumbled.

Rachel and Kirsty darted up and hovered in front of him.

"We know you've been hiding Kathryn's magical badge in your sneaker," said Rachel. "Please give it back. It doesn't belong to you."

Kirsty flew over
to join Rachel
and Kathryn.
They were
all feeling
worried. They
had to get
the badge back
soon, or tomorrow's
gym class would be a disaster. Suddenly,
Kirsty had an idea. She nudged her
friends and then smiled at the goblin.

"You were really good at the obstacle
course," said Kirsty. "You must be a
really talented athlete."

Kathryn looked a little confused, but
Rachel instantly guessed what her best
friend was trying to do.

"I don't think he's that good," she said to Kirsty. "I bet he couldn't jump over this muddy ditch."

Kirsty hid a smile. The ditch was much too big for anyone to jump over.

"Of course he could," she said. "Easy peasy!"

"No, I don't believe it," said Rachel, shaking her head and looking at the goblin.

He laughed and puffed out his chest.

"Of course I could jump over a silly little ditch!" he boasted. "I could do it with my eyes closed."

"Prove it," said Kathryn.

The goblin took a few steps back. Then he squeezed his eyes shut, took a running leap, and landed in the mud with an enormous SPLASH!

"WAHHH!" he yelled.

With filthy water dripping down his face and clothes, he squelched out of the ditch, his sneakers oozing mud.

"That was your fault!" he grumbled.

"Maybe you should take off those muddy shoes," Kirsty suggested.

The three friends crossed their fingers. Would their plan work?

A Magical Inspection

The goblin shook his head. He sat down on the edge of the ditch and hugged his knees, looking very unhappy. Rachel, Kirsty, and Kathryn flew down and landed in front of him.

"Kathryn, could you use your magic to make him some new sneakers?" Rachel asked.

Kathryn waved her wand, and a pair of glittery green sneakers appeared in front of the goblin. They had zig zags down each side, and tiny lights flickered around the soles. The goblin's mouth fell open—he had never seen anything so wonderful!

"Why don't you swap your old sneakers for these new ones?" asked Rachel. "I'm sure they would fit you perfectly."

The goblin was already pulling off his muddy shoes. He flung them aside and pushed his enormous feet into the new ones. Kathryn dived toward the old sneakers and plucked out a muddy, slightly wet golden badge. It instantly

shrank to fairy size,
and Kathryn
polished it
against her
pants until it
gleamed.

"Yes!"
cheered Kirsty.

The goblin
didn't even notice
that he had lost the
badge. He couldn't take his eyes off his
sparkling new sneakers. Rachel grabbed
Kirsty's hands and they twirled around,
spinning into the air. Kathryn sent a
stream of fairy dust swirling around them
and they sank downward, growing back
to human size. Suddenly they were on
the ground, still twirling.

"We did it!" said Rachel. "We got the last badge back!"

"You've both been wonderful!" said Kathryn. "Thank you from the bottom of my heart!"

She gave them each a fluttery kiss on the cheek, and waved her hand. Then, in a flash of sparkles, she returned to Fairyland.

"Now there's just one problem left," said Kirsty. "We have to prove to Mrs. Best that we can complete that obstacle course!"

The next morning, bright and early,
Mr. Beaker's class was back out on the
field in their gym uniforms. Mr. Beaker
had set up the obstacle course, and Mrs.
Best was watching from the side. Rachel
and Kirsty were standing beside the goblins
and overheard them muttering to each
other.

"I don't want to do this anymore,"
said the goblin with the new green
sneakers. "Without that badge, we'll be
as ordinary as these silly humans."

"Let's sneak away and skip it," said the
second goblin.

Kirsty leaned closer to them.

"Just give it a chance," she whispered.
"This is supposed to be fun—you don't
have to be the best to enjoy yourselves,
you know!"

The next half hour was filled with squeals of delight, laughter, and cheering. It was a completely different class from the day before. Everyone did well on the obstacle course, and Mrs. Best kept nodding and smiling. The goblins seemed to enjoy it, too, even though they tripped over their own feet a few times.

"Good effort, you boys in green!"
called out Mrs. Best. "Excellent work,
everyone!"

The class helped to clean up the
equipment and then went to get
changed. Rachel and Kirsty were the last
to pile up their cones.

"That was so fun,"
said Rachel. "I
love gym!"

"PSSST!"

The girls
looked around,
puzzled.

"What was that?" asked Kirsty.

"PSSST!"

The girls looked down and saw
Kathryn peeking out from behind the
cones and beckoning to them.

"Kathryn!" said Rachel. "I didn't think we'd see you again so soon!"

"I've come to invite you to the Fairyland School," she said. "We're in the middle of the royal visit, and it's going really well—thanks to you! We think you should be there, too."

The girls looked over their shoulders. The rest of their class was walking away from them, and Mr. Beaker and Mrs. Best were talking to each other. Rachel and Kirsty exchanged an excited look. They knew that no time would pass in the human world while they were gone.

"We'd love to come!" said Kirsty.

A few minutes later, the girls were following Queen Titania and King Oberon around the Fairyland School. Marissa, Alison, Lydia, and Kathryn were leading the way and looking very proud.

"This is our library," said Lydia, opening the door to a large, quiet room filled with books. "Fairies can come and read the books whenever they want. As you can see, there are always lots of students in here."

Many young fairies were curled up in squishy armchairs, reading or fluttering around the enticing shelves. The king and queen smiled.

"You are running a very happy school," said King Oberon. "Every class we have seen has been fun and interesting. It makes *me* want to go back to school!"

Everyone laughed, and the girls squeezed each other's hands. They knew that the visit was going so smoothly because the School Day Fairies had their magical badges back.

"Finally, we would like to show Your Majesties a gymnastics class," said Kathryn.

She led them all to the auditorium, where the fairy gymnastics class was waiting. When they saw the king and queen, they began their synchronized flying routine. It was incredible! They twirled and spun through the air,

performing the same moves in perfect
harmony without a single mistake.

"They're amazing!" said Kirsty with a
gasp.

Just then there was a knock on the
auditorium door, and Kathryn hurried
to open it. The girls saw her gasp
and step backward. Jack Frost and a
crowd of goblins were walking into the
auditorium!

A Demonstration and a Display

The School Day Fairies were so shocked that they couldn't speak, but Queen Titania stepped forward.

"Why are you here, Jack Frost?" she asked in her gentle voice. "You have caused a lot of trouble for the School Day Fairies this week. I hope that you have not come to make more mischief."

Jack Frost jerked his thumb over his shoulder at the goblins.

"These goblins are so ungrateful," he complained. "I've been trying to teach them all about me and how great I am, but they just don't want to listen."

"The Fairy School has trampolines!" piped up one brave goblin.

"We want to play with all this stuff," added another, waving his arm at the gym equipment.

The School Day Fairies smiled at them.

"You're all very welcome here," said Kathryn. "We love finding new students."

The goblins jumped up and down in excitement, and rushed forward to join the gymnastics class. Soon they were jumping on trampolines and leapfrogging over the vault. Kathryn was a good teacher, and she made sure that they all behaved well and took turns.

"Look," Rachel exclaimed. "I think Jack Frost wants to join in!"

He had been edging closer to the gym equipment. Suddenly he threw off his cloak and did ten somersaults across the mats without stopping. The fairies burst into applause, and Jack Frost grinned and bowed several times. Kathryn came over to the girls, smiling.

"I think Jack Frost is figuring out that school can be fun!" she said, her eyes sparkling.

"Thank you for bringing us here," said Kirsty.

"It's been wonderful to see you again," said Lydia, joining them.

Marissa and Alison came over, too, and they all shared a big hug.

"Thank you again for every- thing you've done," said Kathryn. "We have to send you back to the human world now, but I hope we'll see you again soon."

The fairies waved good-bye. Then, in a flurry of sparkles, the girls found themselves back on their own school field beside the cones. Mr. Beaker and Mrs. Best were still talking and the other students were still walking back into the school. No time had passed at all.

"Come on," said Rachel. "I want to enjoy every second of our last day at school together!"

That afternoon, all the Tippington students gathered in the auditorium to present their displays. Every class had added different things. Mrs. Best examined all of the work and wrote lots of notes on her clipboard.

"Mr. Beaker looks as nervous as I feel!" said Rachel, seeing the teacher biting his lip.

Maya, Dylan, and Zac's model train was on display from the art lesson, along with book reports from the entire class. Rachel and Kirsty had added a picture of a plant from the science lesson.

As Mrs. Best was reading some of the book reports, Kirsty looked around and nudged her best friend.

"Did you notice that the goblins have left?" she asked in a low voice.

"They must be back in Fairyland," said Rachel. "I bet they didn't like our school when they couldn't use the magical badges!"

At last, Mrs. Best reached the end of the display, and turned to face the pupils. She looked down at her clipboard and then gave a big smile.

"I am happy to say that I am very impressed with you all," she said. "Your teachers are inspiring, your work is superb, and your manners are excellent. I am delighted to announce that Tippington School is outstanding!"

Everyone cheered and clapped—even the teachers! Rachel and Kirsty hugged each other.

"I wish you were staying here," said Rachel, holding her best friend tightly.

"Me, too," said Kirsty, feeling a little sad. "It will seem strange to be back at Wetherbury School next week. But it's already been a magical time, hasn't it?"

"It's always magical spending time with you," said Rachel. "And I can't wait until our next fairy adventure!"

RAINBOW magic

Rachel and Kirsty found the School
Day Fairies' missing magic badges.
Now it's time for them to help

Giselle
the Christmas Ballet Fairy!

Join their next adventure in this
special sneak peek...

Best Friends Forever

"It's Christmas Eve," said Rachel Walker, gazing out of her bedroom window at the snowy sky. "Santa Claus and his elves are packing the sleigh full of toys, the reindeer are getting ready for their journey..."

"...and we are going to have the most amazing day ever," finished her best friend, Kirsty Tate.

Rachel turned and smiled at her.
The one thing that made Christmas
truly perfect was being able to share
it with each other. This year was
especially exciting, because the girls had
received a wonderful early Christmas
present. Months ago they had entered a
competition called Best Friends Forever.

They had had to draw a picture of
each other and write one hundred words
about what made their best friend special.
They had forgotten all about the competition until a typed white envelope arrived,
addressed to them both.

Dear Rachel and Kirsty,

Congratulations! We are delighted to tell you that you have won first prize in our Best Friends Forever competition.

Your description of your magical friendship is inspiring, and we all feel that you deserve a special day out together.

You told us that you both love dancing, so we have arranged for you to spend a day at the famous Castle Springs Ballet School.

We have also included two tickets for the evening performance of *Swan Lake*.

Have a wonderful Christmas and enjoy spending time together.

Best wishes,

Amanda Blake

Amanda Blake
Competition Manager

RAINBOW magic™

Which Magical Fairies Have You Met?

- ❏ The Rainbow Fairies
- ❏ The Weather Fairies
- ❏ The Jewel Fairies
- ❏ The Pet Fairies
- ❏ The Dance Fairies
- ❏ The Music Fairies
- ❏ The Sports Fairies
- ❏ The Party Fairies
- ❏ The Ocean Fairies
- ❏ The Night Fairies
- ❏ The Magical Animal Fairies
- ❏ The Princess Fairies
- ❏ The Superstar Fairies
- ❏ The Fashion Fairies
- ❏ The Sugar & Spice Fairies
- ❏ The Earth Fairies
- ❏ The Magical Crafts Fairies
- ❏ The Baby Animal Rescue Fairies
- ❏ The Fairy Tale Fairies
- ❏ The School Day Fairies

📖 SCHOLASTIC

HiT entertainment

Find all of your favorite fairy friends at
scholastic.com/rainbowmagic

RMFAIRY

RAINBOW magic™

Magical fun for everyone! Learn fairy secrets, send friendship notes, and more!

HiT entertainment

www.scholastic.com/rainbowmagic

RMACTIV4

RAINBOW magic™

SPECIAL EDITION

Which Magical Fairies Have You Met

- ❏ Joy the Summer Vacation Fairy
- ❏ Holly the Christmas Fairy
- ❏ Kylie the Carnival Fairy
- ❏ Stella the Star Fairy
- ❏ Shannon the Ocean Fairy
- ❏ Trixie the Halloween Fairy
- ❏ Gabriella the Snow Kingdom Fairy
- ❏ Juliet the Valentine Fairy
- ❏ Mia the Bridesmaid Fairy
- ❏ Flora the Dress-Up Fairy
- ❏ Paige the Christmas Play Fairy
- ❏ Emma the Easter Fairy
- ❏ Cara the Camp Fairy
- ❏ Destiny the Rock Star Fairy
- ❏ Belle the Birthday Fairy
- ❏ Olympia the Games Fairy

- ❏ Selena the Sleepover Fairy
- ❏ Cheryl the Christmas Tree Fairy
- ❏ Florence the Friendship Fairy
- ❏ Lindsay the Luck Fairy
- ❏ Brianna the Tooth Fairy
- ❏ Autumn the Falling Leaves Fairy
- ❏ Keira the Movie Star Fairy
- ❏ Addison the April Fool's Day Fairy
- ❏ Bailey the Babysitter Fairy
- ❏ Natalie the Christmas Stocking Fairy
- ❏ Lila and Myla the Twins Fairies
- ❏ Chelsea the Congratulations Fairy
- ❏ Carly the School Fairy
- ❏ Angelica the Angel Fairy
- ❏ Blossom the Flower Girl Fairy
- ❏ Skyler the Fireworks Fairy

3 stories in each one!

SCHOLASTIC

Find all of your favorite fairy friends at
scholastic.com/rainbowmagic

HIT entertainment

RMSPECIAL